Given by
Diane Saunders

Spring 1990

A Hundred Scoops of Ice Cream

Design by Mary Mietzelfeld

ISBN: 0-312-01444-9
LCC: 87-27451

First Edition
10 9 8 7 6 5 4 3 2 1

ndred
Scoops of
Cream
T A L E S

by
NATASHA
JOSEFOWITZ

Drawings by
MARY
MIETZELFELD
SIEGEL

St. Martin's Press
New York

A Parents

There are small pleasures and small problems which occur every day of a child's life, like having an imaginary friend or brushing teeth. Then there are the pleasures and problems which happen only sometimes, like playing in the ocean or being afraid of the dark. And finally, there are those events which children experience only once a year, like birthdays, or once in a lifetime, like the very first day of school.

These short tales are celebrations of the events in a child's life. They are written in the voices of children, so that every child can point to himself or herself, nod in recognition, and say, "That's me!"

Any way that you read this book with your children is the right way. My own experiences in reading these poems to my grandchildren lead me to offer a few suggestions that may help you and your children to enjoy these tales even more.

Note For

For instance, you may want to stop after some of the poems and talk together about how they apply to life in your family. There may be feelings your listeners want to share, and questions they want to ask. My grandchildren frequently say, "Read it again." It's important to do so. A child may ask for several repetitions. Respecting the child's own rhythms in absorbing the stories is also important.

You probably already know that children love a lot of dramatic inflection when they're read to. In "Bedtime," it's nice to yawn at the end and pretend to fall asleep. You may also want to personalize the poems, substituting your child's age in "Birthday," the name of a friend your child knows in "New Bike," and "sister" or "brother" wherever appropriate.

However you read this book, you'll want to linger over the tales with your children. Maybe they'll even trigger some of your memories, and you can share stories of your own childhood with your children. This book is to help you enjoy each other in your continuous, evolving relationship, to make telling each other tiny tales, and talking about what you're thinking and feeling, a bigger part of your lives.

When my children were small, our bedtime rituals included a story about the various events of their day. Some days it would be about little things, like what they had for supper; other days it was bigger matters, such as temper tantrums. Sometimes I would sing the story. This gave us an opportunity to talk about what happened and share feelings.

Although I have written books on management and humorous verse for adults, writing for children had not occurred to me until I started telling my five grandchildren stories about their days, putting some of the events in verse form. To my surprise, they wanted these stories repeated over and over. The different grandchildren all had different favorites. I also tested the 50 or so poems on many other children. I listened to their comments, watched their expressions, talked to their parents, and followed their suggestions.

Came
this
Book

These stories began to take shape as a book through the encouragement of my agent, Ruth Cohen, and the support and helpful comments of my editor, Janet Vultee, who turned out to be a poet in her own right and a joy to work with. I am grateful to them both.

I also wish to thank Kati Mikes-Papp, my administrative assistant and my sounding board, who listened to the verses, made suggestions, typed them, filed them, retyped them and refiled them many times, always with good cheer.

In addition, my friends' children and grandchildren have been most helpful in listening to these verses and commenting on the ones they liked most and least. I trusted their feedback and made the changes they suggested. I wish to acknowledge the following children for their help:

Marejka and Geoffrey Shaevitz   Lauren Polis
Alexander and Nicky Gourevitch   Noelle and Nicole Sadler
Shazara Max Bloomfield   Jessica Snyder
Jordana and Jorian Polis-Schutz   Julie Glazer
Christina, Isabel, and Elena Nicod Jamie Tamkin

Dedication
xx's
+ oo's

FOR

my granddaughter, Laura, who is 8 and
her brother Aaron, 9 months old;
and for
my grandson, Nicholas, who is 4½,
and for
my step-grandsons, Eliot, who is almost 5,
and his brother Nicky, who is 1½.

This book speaks in their voices.
They inspired these verses, and then with
their suggestions, improved
them.
I thank them all for both.

N. J.

for
Miles
and for my family, old + new

M. M. S.

Every Day
Little Pleasures
and
Little
Problems

growing

I don't feel
me
growing taller,

but I can see
my pants
growing shorter.

My Special House

I put two chairs upside down

on the floor,

and put a blanket over them

to make a tent.

I crawl in

and just sit there.

It's my house.

Sometimes I take my animals in

and pretend I'm feeding them.

Sometimes I'm an Indian chief

who plays the drums.

Sometimes I'm a baby

and suck my thumb.

Sometimes I'm a lion

and I make roaring noises.

I can be anything I want

in my own special house.

Superman OR Wonderwoman

If I wanted to,
I could climb up
to the roof of my house.

If I wanted to,
I could swim all the way
across the lake.

If I wanted to,
I could jump
from the top
of the tallest tree.

If I wanted to,
I could run faster
than anyone
in the whole school.

If I wanted to,
I could take the bus
across town alone,

But I decided that
I don't really want to,
not today anyway.

Lapsitting

I'm too little

to go to the movies.

I'm too small

to eat with the guests.

I'm too young

to stay up late,

But I'm just the right size

to sit on my mommy's lap.

When I Grow Up

When I grow up,
I'm going to be
a firefighter.
A doctor?
An astronaut?
A teacher?
A police officer?
A rock singer?
A mail carrier?

I really don't know
what I'm going to be
when I grow up!

Riding Tall

I don't mind sitting in a stroller,
especially when I'm tired.
I also like to walk
and even better
I like to run.

But best of all
I like to ride
on my daddy's shoulders
while I hold on to his head
and see everything
from way up high.

Sometimes my daddy gallops
like a horse,
and I bounce up and down,
which makes me laugh.

When I'm on my daddy's shoulders
I can touch the tree branches,
and I can almost reach the sky.

When I'm up high
on my daddy's shoulders
I am the tallest of all.

I'm Supposed To

I'm supposed to say "please"
and "thank you."
I'm supposed to
stand straight,
sit quietly
and not mumble.

I'm not supposed to shout,
slam doors,
jump on the furniture
or run in the house.

I'm supposed to
pick up my toys
but not bounce my ball
against my bedroom wall.

If I'm supposed to be perfect,
how am I supposed
to have any fun?

My Imaginary Friend

I have a friend who isn't here.
No one knows him but me.

He does everything he wants to—
like eating the whole box of candy
or staying up until very late
and not obeying anyone.

I have a friend who isn't here.
No one knows him but me.

He does all the things
I'm not supposed to do,
my friend who isn't here.

I Like School

I like school
and I don't like school
all at the same time.

I like school
because I play with my friends
and paint pictures
and sing
and my teacher is nice.

I don't like school
because my little sister
gets to stay home
with Mommy all day
while I am away.

I wish I could
go to school
and stay home
at the same time.

Bathtub

I don't know why I have to be clean,
I don't mind being dirty.

I don't like to have to take a bath,
but I like playing in the bathtub.

I hate to have my hair washed,
but I love blowing soap bubbles.

What I like best
is getting wrapped up in
        my big towel,
and getting a good rub
to dry me off.

Bedtime

Mommy
I'm not tired.
Read me one more story.

Mommy
It's too dark.
Leave the door open.

Mommy
I'm thirsty.
May I have a glass of water?

Mommy
Find my slippers.
I have to go to the bathroom.

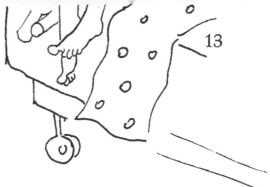

Mommy
Sit with me.
I'm afraid of bad dreams.

Mommy
I'm so hungry.
Can you get me a cracker?

Mommy
Please get my teddy bear.
He fell off the bed.

Mommy
Don't go.
Sing me another song.

Mommy
I'm not sleeepeee . . . .

Mommyyy . . . .

When my room
is dark at night,
I see goblins
sitting on my toy chest.

And ghosts are moving
behind my curtains,
and witches are peering
through the windows,

I'm Afraid of the

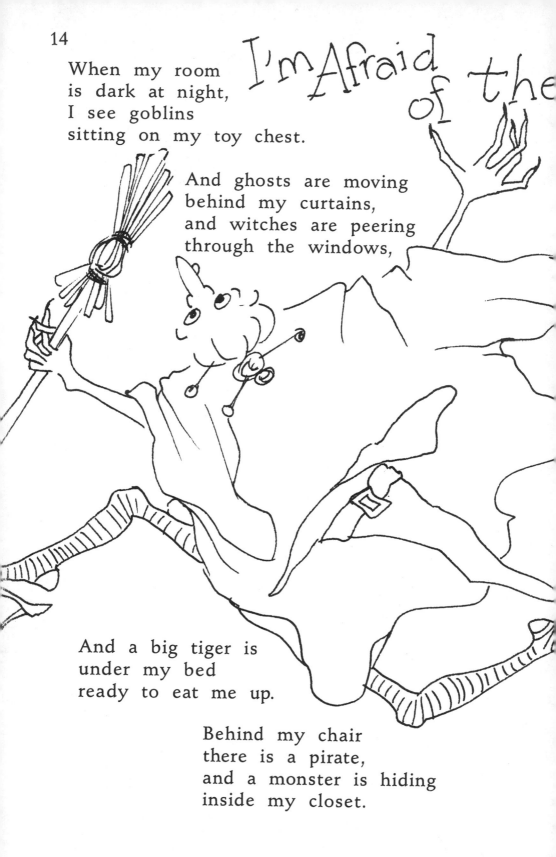

And a big tiger is
under my bed
ready to eat me up.

Behind my chair
there is a pirate,
and a monster is hiding
inside my closet.

And if I make the
slightest noise,
they will all pounce on me.

So I lie in bed,
afraid to move,
afraid to breathe.

But if the light is turned on
in the hall,
and my door is open
so I can see,

Then the witches and the pirates,
the tiger and the monster,
the goblins and the ghosts
all disappear.

I guess they must be even
more afraid of the light
than I am afraid of the dark.

15

Sugar Mountain

I like lots of sugar
on my cereal.

My mother says it's bad
for my teeth.

Every morning we argue.
She says just *one* spoon.

So I get a big soup spoon,
but she takes it away.

So I put a mountain of sugar
in my small spoon.

But my mother gets angry
and I won't eat my cereal.

So my mother lets me have
a small hill of sugar on my spoon
and I eat my cereal all up.

Brushing Teeth

Why do I have to
brush my teeth?
It's sooo boring.

My father explains
about cavities
but that doesn't help.

I just don't like to
brush my teeth.
It's boring.

So I do it very fast.
That way, my father has to
brush them again.

When I'm older,
I'll do it right—
by myself.

But for now
it's much more fun
to have him help.

No Fair

I didn't do it.

It wasn't me.

Well ....

It's not my fault.

He started it.

But ....

I couldn't help it!

I didn't mean it!

And anyway ....

It just happened
by itself.

I won't.

You can't make me.

NO!

I won't obey,
I'm not going,
I won't do it.
I won't clean up.

I won't put away my toys.
I don't want to,
and you can't make me,

so there.

Okay,

I will

if we do it together.

My Best Friend

Who licks my face
when I come home from school?
Who keeps my feet warm
in bed at night?
Who tickles me
with his cold, wet nose?
Who goes for walks
with me in the morning?
Who fetches my baseball
when I throw it too far?
Who protects me
from bullies down the street?
Who eats the vegetables
"dropped" on the floor?

Who does tricks for me
and makes me laugh?

Who is my best friend?

My puppy dog,
that's who!

Sometimes
(Every now &
Then)

I Lost My Bunny Rabbit

I lost my bunny rabbit,
and I can't go to sleep
without him.
I love my bunny.
I tell him secrets.

My sister gives me
her favorite doll.
My brother gives me
his biggest truck.
But I can't sleep
without my bunny.

My mother looks
all over the house.
My father looks
outside in the car.
My grandma finds him
in the garden.

Now I can cuddle
with my own bunny,
and now we can
go to sleep
together.

CLEAN Teddy Bear

My mother washed
my teddy bear.
She said it was filthy.

Now I have
a clean teddy bear.
He doesn't smell
as nice as before.

I liked my dirty
teddy bear better.

A BAD DREAM

I had a bad dream,
and I woke up crying
because I was so scared.

My mommy came into my room,
held me tight,
and said that dreams are not real.

She gave me a sip of water,
tucked me in,
and kissed me good night.

Now I can go to sleep again.
I'm safe, because my mommy
chased my bad dream away.

The BROKEN Lamp

I broke the lamp in the living room.
My ball hit it by accident.
I wasn't supposed to play in the house,
but I did anyway.

Now I'm scared.
My dad will be angry.
Should I say it broke by itself?
Or the cat did it?

But I said it really was my fault,
and my dad hugged me,
because I told the truth.

I promised not to play ball
again in the house.

There is NOTHING to do

I don't have anything to do.
Can Joey come over
to play with me?
  Joey is away for the day, dear.
  Go and play with your toys.
    There's nothing to do.
    Call Sally—
    maybe she can come over?
      Sally has a cold.
      She has to stay home.
      Go and play with your toys.
        Then let's call Robin.
Robin is busy.
Go and play with your toys.
  There is nothing for me to do.
  Will you play with me?
    I can't, dear.
    I have to fix dinner.
    Go and play with your toys.
      No, I want to play with you.
        Let's see.
        Why don't I put
        a big apron on you?
        You can set the table.

Oh, good.
We'll pretend
we're a restaurant.

Old Photographs

I love looking at pictures of myself
when I was a little baby.

I don't remember being so small,
and not able to walk,
or not able to talk.

I also like looking at pictures
of my mommy and daddy
when they were children.

I wish I knew them when they were my age.
We could have been best friends.

Pictures

I drew a picture
of my grandma
and gave it to her.

She put it up
on the refrigerator door
with four magnets

And said it was the best
portrait of her
anyone had ever made.

Picking Up Grandma

My grandma is coming.
I'm really excited.
My grandma is coming!

She's so nice.
She brings me presents
and we play everything I want.

My grandma is coming
and I'm really excited.
We're going to the airport
to pick her up.

When the plane lands,
I hide behind my mommy
just in case
I can't quite remember
what she looks like
exactly.

A Hundred Scoops of Ice Cream

My favorite food
is ice cream—

chocolate with
chocolate chips.

I love it so much
I could eat
a hundred scoops,

but I know I would get
a tummy ache.

So may I please have
just *two*
huge scoops on my cone?

I WON'T Wear My Sweater

I don't want to wear

my sweater today.

My mom says

I can't go out

without it.

I cry,

and throw myself

on the floor,

but she still won't

let me go out without it.

So I open the door,

and pretend

I'm going out anyway.

She closes the door

and gives me a hug.

She says that she loves me

and that's why

I have to wear my sweater today.

So I do.

I love playing
in the ocean.
The water feels
nice and cold and wet.

Playing in th OCE

I'm a little scared
of the waves
but not too much.
It's okay
to be a little scared.

My mother says
I'm getting cold
and should get out.
Not yet.
I'm having
too much fun.

My father says
I'm shivering
and should warm up.
Not yet.
Just one more wave.

My mother says
I've been in
long enough.
It's time to
come out
and dry off.

But I say:
Not yet.
Not yet.
Not yet.

When I see a little puddle
of rain in the street,
I just have to step into it.

When I see a nice big puddle,
I just have to jump in
and make a gigantic splash.

Puddles are there for kids
to have fun in.
Everyone knows that.

But when she sees my wet shoes,
my mommy forgets
that puddles are to have fun in.

I Wish I Had A Puppy

"I wish I had a puppy," I said.
"Well, if not a puppy,
then maybe I can have a kitten?
If I can't have a kitten,
how about a hamster?
No hamster?
Then can I have a canary?
Or maybe a turtle?
Or a little goldfish?"

"Well then,
if no one will buy me an animal,
I'll go get one myself."

So I found a lovely brown worm
and brought it home in a bag
and put it on the dining room table
so he could have dinner with us,
but no one liked my new pet
except me.

The Zoo

Today we're going
to the children's zoo
where we can pet the animals.

But what if they don't like me?

What if the billy goat
bumps me with its horns?

And what if the chicken
pecks me with its beak?

And what if the baby lamb
steps on my toe?

And what if the duckling
snaps at my leg?

And what if the pony
throws me off its back?

Today I'm going to the zoo
where we can pet the animals.

And I'm not really worried
about all the things
that could happen
because if I'm nice to the animals,
they'll be nice to me, too.

In The Mi

Sometimes

not very often

I wake up in the middle of the night.

It's very dark outside,

and I feel lonesome.

I miss my mommy and daddy.

So I take my little blanket

and my teddy bear

and I go to their room.

They are fast asleep

so I sneak into their bed.

Mommy wakes up and says

in a soft voice:

"This isn't your bed.

You must go to sleep in your own bed.

le of the Night

Daddy wakes up and says
in a gruff voice:
"You must go back to your room
right now."

And I say in a tiny little voice:
"I will be very good.
I will be very quiet,
and I want to sleep with you
because I love you."

So my mommy and daddy say
they love me too,
but I have to sleep in my own bed.
And they carry me back,
and tuck me in,
and give me kisses.
And I can go back to sleep
because I'm not lonesome anymore.

I love spaghetti.
It's smooth and wiggly.
I like the way it slides
down my throat.

When I was a baby,
I called it "pasgetti"
but now that I'm older
I can say it right:
"Spaghetti."

I like spaghetti
with lots of cheese.
Sometimes
I put on too much
    and
        it
          gets
            awfully
              s
               t
                r
                 i
                  n
                   g
                    y.

I like macaroni and noodles
and the squiggly shaped pasta
that look like bows and shells
and long flat worms.

I put more and more and more
of it into my mouth
and there is no end to it,
so my daddy has to
cut it up for me
in little pieces.

The Race

I told my dad
I could run
faster than he could.

He said
he didn't
think so.

So I said,
"Let's race."

So we raced.

Well, he did
get there first,

but I *almost* won!

Once In A While
Special Days
+
New Things

The Party Dress

My mommy bought me
a new party dress
and new party shoes
to wear at my birthday
which is next week.

I want to wear them
to school today
but my mommy won't let me.
I promise to be very careful
and not get them dirty
but my mommy says no.

Why can't I wear
my brand-new best party dress
and my beautiful new party shoes
to show my friends
at school today?
I don't understand.

Do you?

The Birthday

Today I'm still only five years old,
but tomorrow I will be six.
I will grow a whole year
in just one day.

My mommy will have a cake for me
with six candles on it
and one for good luck.

My friends are coming over
and Mommy says,
"First we'll play games
and then eat ice cream and cake
and then you'll open all your presents."

I wish I could open my presents first!

Great-Grandpa

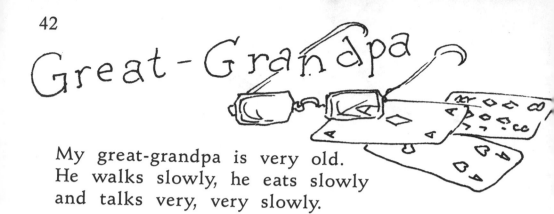

My great-grandpa is very old.
He walks slowly, he eats slowly
and talks very, very slowly.

My great-grandpa falls asleep
in his armchair.
He doesn't like noise
and he won't talk on the phone.

He pats me on the head
and always says
I'm a good child.

He smokes his pipe
and reads his newspaper
and listens to the radio.

And when we play cards,
I always win.

First Movie

My dad took me to a movie.
There were pirates in it.

I got so scared that I cried,
and my dad took me home.

I think I'll go again when I'm older—
maybe next week.

Being SICK

I have a fever.
I feel so hot.
The doctor says
I have to take my medicine
even though it tastes really yucky.

My mommy says I have to
and my daddy says I have to,
but I don't want to, because
it tastes really yucky.

So my mommy puts some honey in it,
and my daddy reads me a story
and they bring me tea with sugar
and dry toast.

And I take the yucky medicine,
because it makes *them* feel better.

Visiting

I'm visiting my grandma
in California for Christmas.
We have snow where I live
but she has sunshine all year long.

I will have to be quiet
in the morning.
I'll have to take a nap after lunch.
I'll have to go to bed early.
I'll have to put away my toys.
I'll have to behave and be good.

She's always saying
it's chilly,
And I can't go barefoot.
I can't leave my blocks
on the floor.
I can't eat cookies
in the living room
and make crumbs.

Grandma

But my grandma takes me to the zoo
and she takes me to the beach.
She takes me out to eat,
and reads me stories
and sings me nice songs.
We dance together
and play pretend games, and
tell riddles and funny jokes.

She hugs me a lot,
and kisses me
and says she loves me
sooooo much!
And even though
I have to be very good
I love my grandma.

First Day of School

This is my first day of school and
I'm getting nervouser and nervouser.

I got up so early
it was still dark outside.
I'm wearing my new school clothes.
My mommy is going with me.

I walk as slowly as I can
and hold on tight to her hand.
The teacher asks my name
but I hide behind my mommy
and won't tell her.

I don't want my mommy to go
so I cry and she stays for a while,
but then she has to leave
and I am all alone
even though there are
other children there.

The teacher helps me blow my nose
and wipes my tears.
She gives me paper and crayons
to draw a picture.
She likes it so much
that she puts it on the wall.

I play with the other children
and eat lunch: my favorite,
peanut butter and jelly sandwich.
I take a nap and play some more.
When my mommy comes to pick me up
I don't want to go home.

The New Bike

I hate Sally.
She was my very best friend yesterday
but today she said she hated me
because I won't let her
ride my brand-new bike.

Tomorrow when it's an old bike,
I'll let her ride it.
So tomorrow Sally will play with me
and be my very best friend again.

NEW
MINE
ONLY

The Injection

I'm scared.
I have to have a shot.
The doctor is going to do it.
He says it's only going to hurt
a tiny little bit,
but I know it's going to hurt
a terrible, terrible lot.

So I squeeze my mommy's hand
and I say: "Wait a minute.
I'm not ready."
But the doctor says: "Now"
and then I feel a little prick.

I wait for it to hurt terribly
and then the doctor says:
"It's all over."

I'm so surprised
because it was just
like a little pin prick.

Everyone said
I was very brave.

The New Baby

My mommy just had a baby.
Everybody says he's so cute.

I think he's ugly and stupid
so there!

He doesn't have any hair, or any teeth.
He can't talk, and he can't play with me.

I wish my mommy would have had
a baby my own age.

Christmas

Tomorrow is Christmas.
I'm so excited,
I can't sleep.
Santa Claus will come tonight
and put toys underneath the tree.
I'm going to stay up
and hide behind the door
to watch him.

I hear a noise.
It must be Santa Claus
but I'd better not go down
and peek.
What if he saw me
and got scared
and ran away
and didn't leave me any toys?

Losing A Tooth

I lotht a tooth.
   I can't thpeak right—
I thound funny.
   And when I thmile,
I look funny, too.

Thoon I will have
a brand-new tooth,
bigger and thtronger
than the one I lotht

But I will mith
thticking my tongue
in the hole.

The Band Aid

I have a boo-boo on my finger.
No one else can see it,
   but I can.

   It's a tiny little spot,
   but it hurts.

   If I put a Band Aid on it,
it disappears.

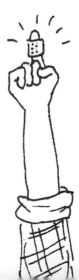

Natasha

Dr. Natasha Josefowitz has had many years of experience working with parents and children as part of a therapeutic team in a child guidance clinic. She is currently an adjunct professor at the College of Health and Human Services at San Diego State University. She is also a nationally syndicated columnist, a well-known lecturer, and the author of:

Paths to Power—A Woman's Guide from First Job to Top Executive (Addison-Wesley, 1980)
You're the Boss—Managing with Effectiveness and Understanding (Warner Books, 1985)
Fitting in: How to Get off to a Good Start in a New Job (Addison-Wesley, 1988)

Poetry:

Is This Where I Was Going?
    (Warner Books, 1983)
Natasha's Words for Families
Natasha's Words for Friends
Natasha's Words for Lovers
    (Warner Books, 1986)

Mary

Mary Mietzelfeld Siegel grew up in and around New York City, reading and sketching. She graduated from Williams College where she concentrated in English and Art History. Over the years she has won close to thirty awards and honors for her illustration and design. She illustrated the *Natasha's Words* trilogy last year. This is her first book for children. She loves ice cream.